SPECIAL THANKS

To my readers, continue to dream big! Reading opens doors that are beyond our imagination, giving way to new creations and unexpected possibilities.

To my Mom and Dad, my sister Chantelle and brother Brandon, thank you for the encouragement and unconditional love and support!

Also, my grandfather Arthur Turner, thank you for your guidance and inspiration.

THE DAY MOHAN FOUND HIS CONFIDENCE

AUTHOR: *ANAYA LEE WILLABUS*

PHOTOGRAPHS BY: CHANTELLE TEEKASINGH

EDITED BY: RAJMATIE WILLABUS

RHYTHM NATION PUBLISHING

MAY, 2015

PRINTED IN THE USA

CONTENTS

CHAPTER 1
THE FIRST DAY

It was a different feeling at Public School 1102 as Mohan entered his new class. He was greeted with a smile from his new teacher, Mrs. Gladfew. She introduced him to the class, but as he walked towards his seat, Peter stuck his foot out to trip him. Some of the children laughed and Mohan sensed that he was going to have to earn his friendship, as well as, manage the experiences of a challenging third grade year, at a new school.

Mrs. Singh, Mohan's mom, knew something was wrong when he called to confirm getting home safely from school. His tone of voice said everything. She tried to find out what was on his mind, but her boss called her to perform a task. *"Why me, why me?"* Mohan cried out. *"I am so tired of moving and changing schools!"* Nobody was around to hear his desperate cry. Grandma Celeste was sound asleep in her room. Mohan cried himself to sleep on the couch. The slamming of the door woke him at almost 12:45 am. Mrs. Singh had just returned home from work. She had to work two jobs to support her son and mother-in-law.

At 5:45 the next morning, the alarm went off and Mohan sprung up to prepare for his second day of school. After showering, Mohan realized he had not completed his homework. Mohan had some trouble understanding the topic. Usually, his mom would review his assignments; however, she had not seen his homework from the night before. This was a pattern that repeated itself.

By the time Mohan was dressed, Mrs. Singh was already prepared for work. She kissed Mohan on his forehead, wished him a productive day and rushed out the door.

Grandma Celeste sat with Mohan, encouraging him to eat his oatmeal as he slumped over the kitchen table. As he ate, Grandma Celeste asked Mohan if his homework was complete, but when he showed her the unfinished workbook, she was unable to assist him. She apologized and explained that as a child in Guyana, Math was done differently. Grandma Celeste went on to explain, "*I could barely remember my multiplication tables now*!"

Mohan finished up his breakfast and rushed to catch the bus to school. Shortly after he entered his class, Mrs. Gladfew collected everyone's homework. Throughout the day Mohan struggled to complete his classwork in a timely manner.

A little before dismissal, Mrs. Gladfew called Mohan to inform him that she did not receive his workbook. Mohan stated that he forgot it at home, so she told him to bring it in the next day.

Friday morning had arrived, still no homework had been submitted and Mohan was still struggling to keep up. Mrs. Gladfew had no choice, but to call Mrs. Singh. Unfortunately, Mrs. Singh never returned the calls and did not respond to the notes sent in Mohan's backpack. Mrs. Gladfew was under the impression that Mrs. Singh was ignoring her. She gave Mohan the weekend to catch up on all his unfinished school work. He promised to complete everything by Monday.

CHAPTER 2

THE SPECIAL ANNOUNCEMENT

Monday came around and everyone was sharing things they did with their family during the weekend. Mrs. Gladfew had stepped out of the class for a few minutes. Collette and Mohan used the opportunity to chat. Collette talked about her upcoming family vacation to her mother's homeland, Guyana. Collette had a priceless gaze on her face as she described all the things she planned on doing. She barely took a breath as she rattled off her list of activities, *"drinking coconut water at Big Market, eating sugar cane, flying kites at the National Park, visiting the zoo, cherry picking..".* The list seemed endless!

Collette spoke of the approaching Easter season and she told Mohan that children would fly kites that were as small as a finger or as big as a truck. Mohan had a gut full of laughter in response. He told Collette that there was no such thing as a kite so small, but he did enjoy her story. She argued that it was true and that her mom grew up doing those same things.

Collette went on to mention a story, told by her mom, about a little girl that held a kite so big that after it went up in the air, the kite lifted her off her feet. The family chased after the little girl as she flew about. Just as she was blown away, her dad grabbed her by the legs, bringing her safely back to the ground.

Mohan was so inspired by Collette's story that he decided to share one of his. It was a story that his grandmother had told him about a little boy who grew up to be a great role model. He was so poor that he had no shoes, but like many other children in Grandma Celeste's village, he did not allow this to be an excuse to miss school.

Many years later, the little boy grew up to be a doctor who often visited his hometown and always donated food and clothing to the less fortunate.

Mohan proudly stated, "*My grandmother always encourages me to stay focused and take my education seriously.*" She said, *"one day, I will be someone great!"*

"*It's been nice talking with you, Collette.*" said Mohan. Collette agreed and asked, "*Would you like to have a play date this weekend?*" Mohan replied, *"I think that should be fine!"* "*I just have to ask my mom.*" Collette looked happy.

Mrs. Gladfew came back into the classroom with an important announcement. The schools in the Mill Basin area of Brooklyn were asked to raise funds towards the purchase of one hundred books for their school's library. The school that raised the most money would also receive additional prizes. The children were all very excited to hear the news.

Principal Bartfort came into the classroom to announce his support of the fundraising event. He mentioned to the class that the school would be hosting a fun day as a way to raise money.

The fun day would be held on a Sunday so that parents could be part of the festivities. *"Boys and girls, I want you to showcase your hidden talents!" "I know many of you dance, play instruments, sing, or play sports." "I cannot wait to see how well each of you will do!"*

As the principal went on, Mohan's mind began to wonder. It was filled with the stories and memories of his hero, his dad.

CHAPTER 3
YOUNG SINGH

Mohan reflected on the days of playing soccer with his dad in their backyard. Mr. Singh was the captain and a midfielder for the Brooklyn Arrowhead Team. He played soccer all his life as a child in Guyana.

The skills of playing soccer came naturally because the neighborhood children had nothing better to do in their spare time. They would use an old water coconut to kick around, barefoot, on the old dirt road. When cars passed, everyone paused for safety, then, it would be game time again!

The weather in Guyana was always very hot. After all, it is South America. These games continued over generations. The children did not realize that they were developing a skill that would earn them the possibility of earning a college scholarship or to travel all over the world, representing their country in competition.

One day, after school, a gentleman stopped to watch the children play. He sat there sweating with his white, long-sleeved shirt, tucked into his trousers. He sat for hours in the sun, watching the competitive games unfold. Eventually, the humid weather got to Mr. Jacobs. He had to remove some of his layers of clothing.

At this time, the coconut was taking a thrashing, but it held its own until it took a head shot from young Singh, who scored the final goal. *"Well done, young lads!"* said Mr. Jacobs. *"Who taught you to play that well?"* Young Singh replied, *"Nobody, but myself, sir!"*

Young Singh went on, *"I watch a lot of soccer in my spare time and learned the art and rules of the sport, just like my friends!" "I would like to be as great as the players on my favorite team, Manchester United!"*

Mr. Jacobs was a recruiter from Brazil. He heard about the untapped skills of the boys and wanted to experience it firsthand. He promised to return with good news that would make the boys' parents happy.

Young Singh ran home and told his mother of this mystery man who promised to return and fulfill their dreams of playing soccer internationally. Young Singh's mother laughed and said, *"Promises are made and broken, but let's keep our hopes high my son!"*

Two months had passed and the boys had forgotten all about their saving grace, Mr. Jacobs. Instead, there was the usual debate of who would be climbing the coconut tree to pluck off the next ball. Nobody liked that job, since most of the boys were shirtless and climbing a coconut tree requires a certain skill. Chubby James always felt guilty, since he had the most experience and could get the job done. He would always say, *"This is the last time I tell ya! My skin itches when I climb that tree, not to mention the hairy worms get me, too!"* Everyone enjoyed a good chuckle at his expense.

That afternoon changed everything. Mr. Jacobs came back with a few other men. They sat on the usual spectator's spot, an old lamp post laying on the side of the street corner. The men watched a few games until the weather got the best of them, then their layers started to come off.

Mr. Thomas asked, "*Don't you boys stop for a water break?*" Rawle Joe said, "*No sir, we don't have time to stop for water and besides, we would have to run home for that.*" Mr. Thomas and the other men laughed.

After about an hour of play, the men gathered the boys and told Young Singh, Rawle Joe, Sherwin Todd and Chubby James that they would like to meet their parents. Each boy ran in different directions up and down Princes Street.

A few minutes later the mothers were running, coming to find out what the boys did wrong. Mrs. Todd had her hands on her waist and her face showed that she was readying herself to hear a complaint. Mr. Jacobs started to explain his interest in recruiting the boys and training them for competitive soccer. The boys would compete against children in Guyana, as well as, internationally.

Mrs. Celeste Singh, Young Singh's mother started clapping and asked for more information on how this would work with her son's school schedule. Mr. Jacobs explained that he would arrange a formal meeting with all the children and parents involved to answer all questions. This would be the opportunity of a lifetime for Young Singh and his family, as well as, the other boys.

The boys were very excited to see Mr. Jacobs again. This was the last day, playing soccer was only for fun. The boys knew their future would be brighter and better. The future finally seemed promising!

CHAPTER 4
ONE RAINY DAY

The years went by and Young Singh grew with his friends, playing soccer as their profession. Young Singh simply became Mr. Singh, except to his closest friends.

The pilot training program was so successful that parents all over heard of its success and wanted their children, both boys and girls to enter. Mr. Singh traveled to many countries but nothing would prepare him for the next step in his life.

Mr. Singh met his wife, who was a nurse, and during his many travels they would keep in contact. They got married upon Mr. Singh's return from an international tournament victory.

Mr. Singh's success enabled him to move his family to Brooklyn, New York. They bought a home and life was wonderful. Mr. Singh always prayed for a son and a few years later, Mohan was born.

He wanted his son to follow in his footsteps of being a soccer player. When Mohan was six years old, his dad left to coach a youth league game in Australia.

The morning of the game was unusually cloudy and rainy, however, the weatherman promised it would clear up into a beautiful day. While driving to the soccer arena, Mr. Singh's team bus was struck by another vehicle. Mr. Singh never made it home for Christmas. Things changed a lot for Mohan and his family.

Mohan, his mom and grandma had to move to a smaller place, in a strange part of town and Mrs. Singh took on the task of working two jobs to maintain the home and manage the bills.

Blam...blam....blam, sounded the wood ruler on the desk. *"Wake up boy!"* called out Mrs. Gladfew to Mohan. *"This boy is always day-dreaming."* she muttered.

"Class, as you all heard, Mr. Bartfort has confidence in you!" *"Therefore, it is important that you give your parents the permission form to sign."* *"We want to make this year's fun day the biggest and best since our school has never won and each of you could benefit from the books."*

Mohan's face lit up. He felt a sense of motivation, a sense of belonging. He could do something that he is great at, just like his role model, his dad.

As the days turned to weeks, Mohan tried to improve his ability to complete his homework in a timely manner. He also found, with his new friend Collette's help, he was able to share his feelings with someone. She, in turn, looked at Mohan as someone who she trusted, who listened to her and gave good advice on her own issues.

Mohan was finally able to trust someone and create a sound friendship with Collette. One Saturday, he even came by her house to help her prepare decorations for her church's concert.

Collette and her parents were members of a local Pentecostal Church. Mohan told Collette that he knew nothing much about church but he did know how to pray. Collette laughed and invited Mohan to join her at Sunday school to learn more. Mohan said that he would ask his mom to visit her church one good Sunday.

Mohan told her, "*Thank you for being such a good friend, Collette!*"

"*No, Thank you, Mohan for teaching me about friendship.*" Collette replied.

CHAPTER 5
THE FUN DAY

It was the Friday before the fun day and Mrs. Singh agreed to take Grandma Celeste to support Mohan. Mohan finished eating and started doing his usual soccer drills in the apartment when he broke his mom's glass vase. Grandma Celeste told Mohan to sweep up and start to practice his multiplication tables. Mohan was so excited for Sunday to come that he could barely compose himself. He told his grandmother that he would show off his skills, just like the players of his favorite team, Man. United.

Later that night, as Mohan lay in bed, he could only visualize himself playing soccer. Soccer was the one thing that brought true happiness, an escape from the reality and the worries of the world.

It was Sunday morning and families came out in great numbers. Decorations were everywhere and all the teachers were present with their family. The Mill Basin ball field was crowded. Even the local news team paid a visit. It felt like a day at Coney Island, but without the cotton candy and hot dogs, thought Mohan. Grandma Celeste and Mrs. Singh both showed up with their picnic basket and "dined" in a shaded area.

Mr. Bartfort came up to Mohan and asked him if he would be able to manage all the contests he entered. *"Young man, you entered to sing, play chess, run the bag and track races, and lastly, to take part in the most competitive part of the day, the district soccer match."* Mr. Bartfort asked, *"Are you sure you'll have enough energy for each of these events?"* Mohan excitedly responded, *"Yes Sir, Mr. Bartfort, I can manage, I am about to eat my lunch and get focused."* Curiously, Mr. Bartfort inquired, *"What is for lunch, my boy?"* *"Roti and curry chicken with potatoes, it does the body good, Sir!"* Mr. Bartfort looked at Mohan and laughed. *"I hope so, son!"* *"We always have a tough* time in the soccer match." "I'm hoping this is our year to finally get a victory!"

The games finally unfolded and the other schools brought their best players as PS 1102 tried to hang in. The chess match was won for the first time in eight years because of Mohan. Still, donations were coming in slowly from the parents and other patrons. Mrs. Stones, one of the teachers of PS 1102, took the loudspeaker and pled with everyone to remember the reason for the fun day. "*It is to raise the most funds in the school district so that the school would receive books for the library.*" After she revealed the first win by the chess team, patrons started to increase their donations.

Mohan set off on a winning streak and shot off so fast in that bag race that Sue Faye stopped selling her cupcakes and watched the race. At the finish line, she came up to Mohan and gave him a big hug. *"You are totally awesome!"* said Sue Faye. If that did not give him motivation, then I don't know what would. After all, she is the most popular girl in the school!

Collette stood at the side line and watched as her friend received the stardom he deserved. As Mohan walked with Collette to his mom and grandmother's picnic area, a group of students from one of the other schools threw a few rocks at Mohan. One of them hit him in the head and he fell.

Thankfully, he was examined by the nurse on site and she told him to rest for a little. The soccer game was going to be starting in an hour. Collette told Mohan to take it easy and that he needs to save his strength. This incident caused Mohan to miss the track races and the singing contest. The final and tie-breaking event of the day would be the soccer match.

After resting for a few, the referee called the names of the soccer players. At this time, PS 1102 needed a little more to score the highest in donations. The whistle blew and the game began. The cheering could be heard from every corner of the field.

The competing school principal approached Mr. Bartfort and asked who Mohan was and why he hadn't seen him before. Mr. Bartfort replied, *"He is a new student, my golden savior!"* He continued, *"The boy is unbelievable!"*

It was half time and PS 1102 was tied at 2 points. Mohan seemed tired as he looked for assistance from his fellow teammates. He put together a few plays and his teammates did a great job of working together. Mohan wanted it to be a team effort.

Mohan imagined himself as the captain of the Red Devils, playing the striker position, much like the great Wayne Rooney. Brian, his classmate, was Angel Di Maria, the midfielder. Brian crossed the ball to Mohan.

There were only a few minutes remaining in the game and Mohan felt so tired it was hard to maintain his focus.

Mohan used this opportunity to think of his hero and what he would have done in this position. Mohan could hear his dad's voice cheering him on.

"Let's go tiger, never quit, keep pushing!"

Mohan's mind broke away into the memory of a story. One where his dad talked about the last bit of energy needed to play on and finish a game strongly. Mohan danced around with speed and skill, dribbling the ball around his competitors and struck the ball so hard, it was difficult for the goalie to catch it. Goooaaall!!!

The result was the first ever win for the PS 1102 soccer team! What a victory, yelled the commentator. The news team gathered up their equipment and raced to interview Mohan, but not before Mr. Bartfort grabbed Mohan and hoisted him to his shoulder. *"This is our golden boy!"*

Mohan's smile was so wide he could swallow up all the attention. Mrs. Singh and Grandma Celeste worked their way through the crowd to greet the star of the fun day. The announcement was made that PS 1102 had earned the most donations, so the school would receive the 100 books for the library.

The news reporter asked Mohan, *"How did you learn to master so many things?"* He replied, *"Before my dad passed away, he taught me every sport he knew."* He always said, *"One sport is never enough and you should always challenge yourself to learn new things."*

The reporter asked, *"Do you think your dad would be proud of you?"* Mohan had an amazing smile on his face and responded, *"Not only do I know he is proud of me, but he is always with me in my heart, guiding me."*

The grounds were filled with wet eyes from the inspirational response. The principal, teachers and fellow students all looked at Mohan as the new hero of their school. Collette finally made her way through the crowd with her family to meet Mohan's family. Interestingly enough, Collette's family was from a small village, not so far away from Grandma Celeste's hometown in Guyana.

Mohan ran to the arms of his mom and hugged her so tight. She looked at him and told him how proud she was.

"Let's go home and celebrate!" She ensured Mohan that, *"Your papa is proud of you, too!"*

Mrs. Singh announced to Mohan that she received a promotion at work, so she does not need to work two jobs anymore. Also, Mrs. Singh went on to tell her son that they would be able to spend quality time together since she would be home earlier.

CHAPTER 6
BELIEVE IN YOURSELF

Monday morning could not come fast enough for Mohan. For the first time in a long time, he was truly excited about going to school. He got up, ate his oatmeal and rushed off to school. Mrs. Gladfew was happy to finally meet with Mrs. Singh and smooth out how to best assist Mohan with his schoolwork. Mrs. Singh and Mrs. Gladfew decided they would work together in the best interest of Mohan.

At the morning assembly, Principal Bartfort announced that the new books would be available at the school's library in two weeks for all to read. He went on to talk about the great sportsmanship that he witnessed at the fun day. He called Mohan up onto the stage, along with the other children who partook in the Fun Day's events. Mohan was now well known at his new school as the 'golden boy.'

As Mohan stepped off the stage he felt a warm tingle in his stomach, but he was not hungry. It was the feeling of confidence that was growing. It was the feeling of belonging to somewhere and a sense of appreciation by the other children.

Mohan never knew he could feel so good about himself. He was now doing his homework on time and reviewing it nightly with his mom. Mohan was able to catch up with his classwork and became a better and more positive student. He maintained a true friendship with Collette and they shared many stories and experiences together. All of these things were accomplished in just a few months of learning how to work together with others and appreciate and discover one's true abilities.

Continue to dream big!

Made in the USA
Lexington, KY
15 April 2017

THE
WANTING
SEED

Anthony Burgess

W · W · NORTON & COMPANY

New York · London